HUSH-A-BYE BUNNY

by Holly Surplice

For my little bunnies,

Honey, Coco-Wren & Cherry xxx

H.S.

First published 2016 by Nosy Crow Ltd
The Crow's Nest, 10a Lant Street
London SE1 1QR
www.nosycrow.com

ISBN 978 0 85763 401 6 (HB)
ISBN 978 0 85763 402 3 (PB)

Nosy Crow and associated logos are trademarks and/or registered
trademarks of Nosy Crow Ltd.

A CIP catalogue record for this book is available from the British Library.

Printed in China by Imago

Papers used by Nosy Crow are made from wood grown in sustainable forests.

1 3 5 7 9 8 6 4 2 (HB)
1 3 5 7 9 8 6 4 2 (PB)

HUSH-A-BYE BUNNY

by Holly Surplice

Hush-a-bye Bunny,
The end of the day.
It's time to stop playing
And put toys away.

Hush-a-bye Bunny,
My sweet sleepyhead.
Warm milk and some supper,
It's soon time for bed.

Hush-a-bye Bunny,
With soap on your nose.
Rub-a-dub, scrub-a-dub,
Down to your toes.

Hush-a-bye Bunny,
Now what shall we do?
I'll wrap you up warmly
And play peekaboo.

Hush-a-bye Bunny,
Pyjamas all ready.
First arms in, then legs in,
And snuggle with Teddy.

Hush-a-bye Bunny,
Then let's share a book.
Just cuddle up close
And we'll listen and look.

Hush-a-bye Bunny,
Let's turn out the light.
Now hop into bed
And then let's say goodnight.

Hush-a-bye Bunny,
My darling, don't cry.
Let me rock-a-bye, hush-a-bye,
Tell Mummy why.

Hush-a-bye Bunny,
Now tell me your fears.
I can hug away worries
And kiss away tears.

Hush-a-bye Bunny,
We're never apart.
Wherever you are,
You are here in my heart.

Hush-a-bye Bunny,
The moon is now bright.
I'll love you forever
My bunny . . .

. . . goodnight.